KU-711-854

This book belongs to:

_____

_____

_____

First published 2002 by Walker Books Ltd
87 Vauxhall Walk, London SE11 5HJ

This edition published 2011

2 4 6 8 10 9 7 5 3 1

© 2002 Lucy Cousins
Lucy Cousins font © 2002 Lucy Cousins

"Maisy" Audio Visual Series produced by King Rollo Films for
Universal Pictures International Visual Programming

Maisy™. Maisy is a registered trademark of Walker Books Ltd, London.

The moral right of the author/illustrator has been asserted

Printed in China

British Library Cataloguing in Publication Data:
a catalogue record for this book is available from the British Library

ISBN 978-1-4063-3478-4

www.walker.co.uk
www.maisyfun.co.uk

Maisy Tidies Up

Lucy Cousins

WALKER BOOKS
AND SUBSIDIARIES

LONDON · BOSTON · SYDNEY · AUCKLAND

Maisy is cleaning her house today.

Ding-dong!
Oh, who can that be?

It's Charley!
Come in, Charley.
You're just in time
to help Maisy
tidy up.

Charley can smell something delicious.

What's that in the kitchen, Maisy?

Lots of yummy cakes!

Oh dear, the floor
is still wet.
You'll have to wait
until it's dry, Charley.

While he's waiting, Charley tidies up all the toys.

And Maisy vacuums the sitting room.

Then Charley cleans the windows from the inside...

And Maisy cleans them from the outside.

That looks better!

At last the kitchen floor is dry.
Now Maisy and Charley can have some cakes.
Hooray!

Well done, Maisy.
Well done, Charley.
Enjoy your cakes.

Read and enjoy the Maisy story books

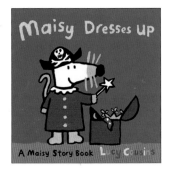

Maisy Dresses Up

A Maisy Story Book Lucy Cousins

Maisy's Bedtime

A Maisy Story Book Lucy Cousins

Maisy's Pool

A Maisy Story Book Lucy Cousins

Maisy Makes Lemonade

A Maisy Story Book Lucy Cousins

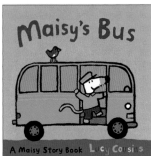

Maisy's Bus

A Maisy Story Book Lucy Cousins

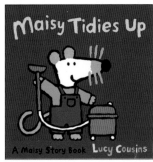

Maisy Tidies Up

A Maisy Story Book Lucy Cousins

Maisy Makes Gingerbread

A Maisy Story Book Lucy Cousins

Maisy's Bathtime

A Maisy Story Book Lucy Cousins

My friend Maisy

Doctor Maisy

A Maisy Story Book Lucy Cousins

Maisy Goes Shopping

A Maisy Story Book Lucy Cousins

Available from all good booksellers

It's more fun with Maisy!